· WILDFLOWERS ·
A TOON BOOK BY
LINIERS
Fig. 71-108

Make sure to find all the TOON books by Liniers:
The Big Wet Balloon, **A *PARENTS MAGAZINE* TOP TEN!**
Written and Drawn by Henrietta, **A BOLOGNARAGAZZI AWARD WINNER!**
Good Night, Planet, **AN EISNER AWARD WINNER!**

TOON LEVEL TWO

For Matilda, Clementina, and Emma

Editorial Director: FRANÇOISE MOULY

Book Design: FRANÇOISE MOULY & RICARDO LINIERS SIRI

RICARDO LINIERS'S artwork was done using India ink and watercolor.

 All our books are Smyth Sewn (the highest library-quality binding available) and printed with soy-based inks on acid-free, woodfree paper harvested from responsible sources.
Library of Congress Cataloging-in-Publication Data: Names: Liniers, 1973- author, illustrator. Title: Wildflowers : a Toon book / by Liniers. Description: First edition. | New York : TOON Books, [2021] | Audience: Ages up to 8. | Audience: Grades 2-3. | Summary: Sisters embark on an adventure of the imagination through the jungles of a mysterious island, which reveals the unbreakable bond they share. Identifiers: LCCN 2020042466 | ISBN 9781943145539 (hardcover) Subjects: LCSH: Graphic novels. | CYAC: Graphic novels. | Sisters--Fiction.| Adventure and adventurers--Fiction. | Imagination--Fiction. Classification: LCC PZ7.7.L56 Wil 2021 | DDC 741.5/973--dc23 Printed in China by C&C Offset Printing Co., Ltd. Distributed to the trade by Consortium Book Sales & Distribution, a division of Ingram Content Group; orders (866) 400-5351; ips@ingramcontent.com; www.cbsd.com.

ISBN 978-1-943145-53-9 (hardcover edition)

ISBN 978-1-943145-54-6 (hardcover special gift edition)

21 22 23 24 25 26 C&C 10 9 8 7 6 5 4 3 2

www.TOON-BOOKS.com

WHERE ARE WE?

THERE WAS A **TERRIBLE** PLANE CRASH!

AND NOW WE'RE STRANDED ON A MYSTERIOUS ISLAND WITH A JUNGLE.

OH, I LOVE JUNGLES! BUT WHAT I LIKE *BEST* IS BUTTERFLIES!
MY FRIEND BILL IS A BUTTERFLY.
MAYBE HE WAS ON THE PLANE?
NO, *CAN'T BE!* BUTTERFLIES DON'T GO ON AIRPLANES.

WE SHOULD EXPLORE THE ISLAND NOW.
LET'S GO!
WAIT FOR ME!

WOW! LOOK AT THESE *EXOTIC* PLANTS!

WHAT DOES *ECK-STO-TICK* MEAN?

IT MEANS VERY, VERY ***WILD***!

HELLO!
YOU ARE SURELY THE STRANGEST WILDFLOWER I HAVE EVER SEEN!
THE FLOWER TALKED TO ME!!

BUT PLANTS DON'T TALK!

THESE DO BECAUSE THEY ARE ECK-STO-TICK BECAUSE THEY ARE IN THE JUNGLE.

DO PLANTS ON THIS ISLAND TALK?
THEY MIGHT.

IT SAID WE ARE FLOWERS, WILD ONES, BECAUSE WE ARE IN THE JUNGLE!

I LOVE BEING A FLOWER.
AND I LOVE BEING WILD!

GRRRR!

GRRR!
GRRR!

ONLY REALITY CAN KILL A DRAGON
O-N-L-
WHAT DOES IT SAY?

"ONLY REALITY CAN KILL A DRAGON." WHAT DO YOU THINK IT MEANS?

I DON'T KNOW. LET'S MOVE ON. WHERE WERE WE?

WE'VE BEEN IN THIS JUNGLE FOR MANY, MANY DAYS NOW.

WE'LL HAVE TO BUILD A SHELTER OR FIND A CAVE.

LOOK!
I FOUND A GORILLA HOUSE!

THAT'S WAY TOO **SMALL** TO FIT A GORILLA!

AND BESIDES, GORILLAS DON'T LIVE ON ISLANDS OR IN HOUSES. WE STUDIED THEM AT SCHOOL.

BUT THIS IS A TINY GORILLA, THE ONLY ANIMAL THAT LIVES ON THE ISLAND. AND IT LIVES IN *THIS* HOUSE.

YOU DON'T KNOW THAT. IT'S NOT *YOUR* ISLAND.
LET'S KNOCK ON THE DOOR.

TOLD YOU!
I ALWAYS WANTED
A POCKET GORILLA!

THIS IS
SILLY!

DID YOU
HEAR THAT?

THAT NOISE...

LIKE A GROWL...

OR **WORSE!**

MAYBE IT'S A GIRAFFE?

A **TINY** GIRAFFE!!!

GIRAFFES DON'T *GROWL*!
AND WE ALREADY HAVE A TINY ANIMAL.

WHAT IS IT THEN? CAN I SAY?

NO!
IT'S A DRAGON!
RUN! RUN!

DON'T SCARE
ME LIKE
THAT.

COME ON!

WAIT
FOR ME!
RUN
AWAY!

WE LOST IT!

FACT: WILDFLOWERS ARE A DRAGON'S FAVORITE FOOD.
THEN IT'S **REALLY** LUCKY WE ESCAPED!

LOOK! IT'S SNOWING!

MMM—IT TASTES LIKE **POPCORN**!

I FEEL SAD.
WHY?
I MISS SOMEONE, BUT I CAN'T REMEMBER WHO.

IT'S THE JUNGLE. IT MAKES YOU FEEL THINGS YOU DON'T UNDERSTAND.

BUT EVEN A SAD FEELING IS AN IMPORTANT ONE.
YES, BUT I DON'T LIKE FEELING SAD.
THEN I THINK WE SHOULD *TICKLE* YOU!

LOOK WHAT
I FOUND!

A REALLY
OLD TEMPLE.

STOP, YOU GUYS!

CAN'T YOU SEE THE SMOKE COMING OUT OF THOSE CHIMNEYS?

DO YOU THINK IT COULD BE...

...THE DRAGON'S...

...LAIR?

IT IS—AAA!!!

HERE IT COMES, HUNGRY FOR A WILDFLOWER BREAKFAST!
HELP US, TINY GORILLA.

AAA!!. IT'S GOING TO EAT MY LEG!

CHOMP
CHOMP
I LOST MY **SHOE**!

G-I-I-I-RLS...
G-I-I-I-I-RLS...

DINNER'S READY, GIRLS.

I WON'T SAY IT AGAIN...
ONLY REALITY CAN KILL A DRAGON

POP CORN
SEA SALT

COME AND SET THE TABLE RIGHT NOW!

OH, BILL. *THERE* YOU ARE!

WAIT FOR ME!

ABOUT THE AUTHOR

"As soon as I took this photo of my three young daughters looking at the jungle in the Yucatan, Mexico, I began to imagine this book," says **RICARDO LINIERS SIRI** about the moment inspiration struck. "Matilda, Clementina, and Emma, 'You belong among the wildflowers,' as the song by Tom Petty goes. Thank you for all that you brought to this story, and thanks to your friend, Paz Babineau, for helping me find the tiny gorilla."

Liniers's U.S. debut, *The Big Wet Balloon*, was selected as one of *Parents Magazine*'s Top Ten, and his second book starring his girls, *Good Night, Planet*, was the winner of the Eisner Award for Best Comics for Beginning Readers. This third book completes the set of the author's ode to his three daughters. Originally from Buenos Aires, Argentina, the family is now happily inhabiting the mysterious jungles of Vermont.